PARENTS AND CAREGIVERS,

Stone Arch Readers are designed to provide enjoyable reading experiences, as well as opportunities to develop vocabulary, literacy skills, and comprehension. Here are a few ways to support your beginning reader:

* Talk with your child about the ideas addressed in the story.

* Discuss each illustration, mentioning the characters, where they are, and what they are doing.

* Read with expression, pointing to each word. You may want to read the whole story through and then revisit parts of the story to ensure that the meanings of words or phrases are understood.

* Talk about why the character did what he or she did and what your child would do in that situation.

* Help your child connect with characters and events in the story.

Remember, reading with your child should be fun, not forced. Each moment spent reading with your child is a priceless investment in his or her literacy life.

GAIL SAUNDERS-SMITH, PH.D.

STONE ARCH **READERS**

are published by Stone Arch Books
A Capstone Imprint
151 Good Counsel Drive, P.O. Box 669, Mankato, Minnesota 56002
www.capstonepub.com

Printed in the United States of America in Melrose Park, Illinois.
092009
005620LKS10

Library of Congress Cataloging-in-Publication data
is available on the Library of Congress website.

Library Binding: 978-1-4342-1873-5
Paperback: 978-1-4342-2306-7

Creative Director: Heather Kindseth
Designer: Bob Lentz
Production Specialist: Michelle Biedscheid

Reading Consultants:
Gail Saunders-Smith, Ph.D.
Melinda Melton Crow, M.Ed.
Laurie K. Holland, Media Specialist

Summary: Snorp needs a break,
so he goes snowboarding.

SNORP

ON THE SLOPES

BY CARI MEISTER

ILLUSTRATED BY
DENNIS MESSNER

STONE ARCH BOOKS
a capstone imprint

SNORP

This is Snorp. He has a very long tongue.

He is the best window washer
in the city.

Wow! Look at the city sparkle!

Snorp's boss is very happy.

"Good work, Snorp!" he says. "You can take tomorrow off. Do something fun."

After dinner, Snorp calls Moopy.

"Hello," he says. "This is Snorp.
I have tomorrow off. Can you
teach me how to snowboard? You
can? Great! See you tomorrow."

In the morning, Snorp packs
his bag. He packs snow pants,
goggles, a book, a toothbrush,
and a box of donuts.

He rides the bus to the mountain. The bus drops Snorp at the bottom of the mountain.

Snorp climbs and climbs.
Then he hears something.

Rustle, rustle.

Something is in the bush!

It is Moopy!

"Nice to see you!" says Snorp.

Moopy does not have eyes.
She cannot see anything.
Instead, she sniffs Snorp.

"Nice to smell you!" says
Moopy.

Moopy sniffs Snorp's bag.
"I smell donuts!" she says.

The two friends sit down for
a snack.

"Now we are ready!" says
Snorp.

The snowboard park is huge.
Snorp has never seen anything
like it.

Suddenly, Snorp is worried. If Moopy cannot see, how can she snowboard?

"Don't worry, Snorp," she says. "I never run into anything."

Moopy pulls a green snowboard from her pack.

"I made this for you," she says. "It has spots for all your feet."

Moopy teaches Snorp how to glide and jump.

She teaches him how to slide and hop.

She does not teach Snorp how to stop.

Oh no! Snorp is going too fast!

Moopy hears Snorp zoom past.

"Stop!" yells Moopy.

"I do not know how to stop!"
yells Snorp.

Snorp cannot stop!

He is going faster and faster.

"Use your tongue!" yells
Moopy.

Oh no!

Poor Snorp. His tongue is stuck to the chairlift!

"Let go!" say the monsters in the chair.

Snorp cannot let go. His tongue is stuck to the metal.

The ski workers come. They pull and pull.

Snorp's tongue is free!

Poor Snorp.

He needs 17 stitches.

Moopy is a good friend. She visits Snorp in the hospital.

She brings flowers and candy.

She sings to Snorp. She hits all the high notes.

Soon, it is time for Snorp to leave the hospital.

Moopy picks him up.

"Are you ready to try again?" she asks.

"Try what?" asks Snorp.

"Snowboarding, of course!" says Moopy.

THE END

STORY WORDS

tongue   donuts   glide

sparkle   mountain   chairlift

snowboard   rustle   hospital

goggles   sniffs

Total Word Count: 397

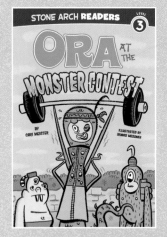

READ MORE MONSTER STORIES!